W9-BEP-825

BIGELOW FREE PUBLIC LIBRARY
CLINTON, MASS.

Spectacular Spain

by

Lisa Thompson

illustrated by

Helen Jones

Editor: Jill Kalz
Page Production: Tracy Kaehler
Creative Director: Keith Griffin
Editorial Director: Carol Jones

First American edition published in 2006 by
Picture Window Books
5115 Excelsior Boulevard
Suite 232
Minneapolis, MN 55416
877-845-8392
www.picturewindowbooks.com

First published in Australia by
Blake Education Pty Ltd
CAN 074 266 023
Locked Bag 2022
Glebe NSW 2037
Ph: (02) 9518 4222; Fax: (02) 9518 4333
Email: mail@blake.com.au
www.askblake.com.au

Printed in the United States of America.

Library of Congress Cataloging-in-Publication Data
Thompson, Lisa, 1969-
Spectacular Spain / by Lisa Thompson ; illustrated by Helen Jones.
p. cm. — (Read-it! chapter books. SWAT)
Summary: Bec and her dog, Bronson, go to Barcelona, Spain, on a Secret World Adventure Team mission to help a famous, but sad, flamenco dancer, and Bec gets some help with her own dancing in the process.
ISBN 1-4048-1675-5 (hardcover)
[1. Adventure and adventurers—Fiction. 2. Dancing—Fiction. 3. Running the bulls—Fiction. 4. Bullfights—Fiction. 5. Barcelona (Spain)—Fiction. 6. Spain—Fiction.] I. Jones, Helen, 1953- ill. II. Title. III. Series.
PZ7.T371634Spe 2005
[E]—dc22 2005027171

Table of Contents

Fact Sheet

Country: Spain
Bordered by: Portugal & France
Language: Spanish
Currency: Euro
Largest Cities: Barcelona
Madrid, Seville, Valen
Customs: Bullfightin
Flamenco Dancing
Food: Paella, Pi
Fabada, Empa
Famous Spa
Pablo Picasso, C
Antonio Gaudi,
El Cid, Goya, Don

Map of Spain
Bilbao
Burgos
Pamplona
Barcelona
Madrid
Valencia
Córdoba
Granada

CHAPTER 1
The Mission

"Turn it down!" Zac screamed, banging on his sister's bedroom door.

"What? Speak up. I can't hear you!" Bec yelled back, twisting and leaping across the room.

Zac stormed in, headed straight for the stereo, and turned the volume down.

"Don't turn the music down," Bec said. "Can't you see I'm dancing?"

"RRRuff! Ruff!" Bronson, Bec's dog, barked in support.

"The whole street has been listening to you play this song over and over for the past two hours. It's driving me nuts!" said Zac.

"I'm practicing for Saturday's dance recital. I only need to play it a couple more times. I've almost got it."

When it came to dancing, Bec was not a natural. Her dance teacher, Miss Kain, would tell the class, "Close your eyes, and feel the music."

Bec would try, but her movements just wouldn't flow. Sometimes she wondered if she was hearing the same music as the rest of the class! She was dreading the recital on Saturday. Getting up in front of a crowd of people and dancing poorly wasn't her idea of fun.

"Just so you won't be tempted, I'll hold on to this for you," said Zac, taking out the CD. Bec tried to argue, but it was too late.

"Great," huffed Bec, falling back on her bed. "Now what am I going to do? I was just getting good at that last bit."

"RRRuff! Ruff!"

It was hard to tell if Bronson was agreeing or not.

"Let's go downstairs and see if I have any e-mail," Bec said.

As Bec danced down the stairs, she tripped, giving her left knee a big red carpet burn.

"Ouch!" Bec hugged her knee. "Classic. Another scar to add to my collection."

Bec thought everything was "classic" at the moment. It was her word of the week. Last week it was "sick," and the week before that, "legendary."

Bec hobbled to the computer. There was only one new e-mail:

> Bec and Bronson, the following information is top secret. Press **ENTER** to proceed.

Bec pressed **ENTER**.

A voice came from inside the computer:

"Hello, Bec and Bronson. My name is Gosic. I am the voice of SWAT, which stands for Secret World Adventure Team. We have a database of every child in the world. This is how we choose our secret agents.

"Congratulations! We have chosen the two of you for our next mission. We urgently need you both in Spain.

"Your mission is to help Paloma Hoyos with her adventure.

"Outside, in Bronson's kennel, you will find two SWAT transporter wristbands. You must wear these wristbands at all times. They allow you to travel in the blink of an eye, and they will keep us in contact.

"Do not tell anyone that you are SWAT agents. Good luck, SWAT."

The screen went blank.

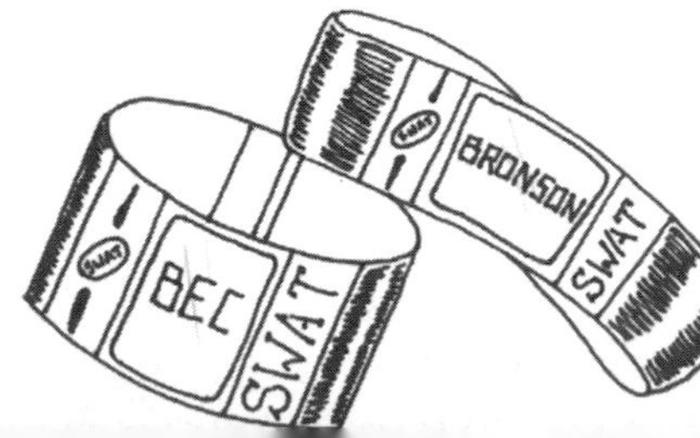

CHAPTER 2

All About Spain

"Excellent! Maybe I'll miss the dance recital." Bec's smile turned to a frown. "This had better not be one of Zac's practical jokes."

Bec and Bronson headed straight for Zac's room and barged in.

"Hey! Don't you knock?" Zac lay on his bed, reading a surfing magazine.

"Sorry, forgot. Zac, what do you know about Spain?" Bec asked.

Zac put down his magazine and looked at the ceiling. "Spain. Let's see. It's in Europe, next to Portugal and just below France. The capital is Madrid. The currency is the euro. It's famous for bullfighting, and everyone speaks Spanish. *Adios!* That's Spanish for 'good-bye.' Now get out of my room."

Zac picked up his magazine and went back to imagining he was surfing huge, tropical waves.

"Adios, dreamer," said Bec, closing the door behind her. "Well, Bronson, it looks like this SWAT mission is for real. Classic! Let's check out your kennel."

The kennel was full of doggy treasures. There were three bones, Bronson's favorite stick, a ball, and a black backpack with SWAT printed in large letters on the side.

"This is it!" cried Bec. "Now let's have a look at these wristbands."

Bronson's was actually a dog collar. Bec's looked like a really cool watch.

Bec slid on her wristband, put the collar on Bronson, and began pulling everything out of the pack. There was a wallet with foreign money in it.

"Look at this, Bronson," said Bec. "This is a euro." Bec held a coin in the air. "We're actually going to Spain! Pretty classic, don't you think?"

Inside the wallet, Bec found a photo of a girl dancing. Her dress was frilly and layered, and she held wooden castanets above her head. In the photo, the bottom of her dress was blurry, like she had been spinning around and around. Her long, dark hair was pulled back tightly, and her dark eyes stared straight at Bec.

"I bet she's a great dancer," Bec said.

Bec turned over the photo. "Paloma Hoyos" was written on the back.

"This is her, Bronson. This is the girl we have to find," Bec said.

She pulled out a copy of the Spanish paper *El Pais*. On the front page, in the bottom corner, was a picture of Paloma Hoyos with the headline "Paloma to Dance at Fiesta."

Bec skimmed the article and noticed the date. "It says here, she is performing in Barcelona tomorrow."

Bec opened the map of Spain and found Barcelona, a large Spanish city.

"Well, Bronson, let's go find Paloma Hoyos." Bec pushed everything into the backpack as she read the instructions. "All we have to do is count down from three and press this button.
Three. Two. One."

Click.

START MISSION.

CHAPTER 3

La Rambla, Barcelona

Bec and Bronson landed in a crowded mall lined with shops, newsstands, cafes, and street performers. Bronson started barking at a man painted bronze who was standing still like a statue. Bec could barely tell he was breathing. A bucket sat at his feet. Bec threw in some euros.

Suddenly, the bronze human statue moved and gave an almighty roar.

"AAAAAAHHHH!" screamed Bec in shock. Bronson went wild, barking and growling.

"Classic!" laughed Bec. "You really scared me—and Bronson!"

But the man did not answer. He went back to acting like a bronze statue until the next coin thrower came along. A crowd had gathered, and Bec noticed a whole bunch of human statues. There was a girl dressed like an alien, two people dressed like ghosts, and someone painted to look like marble.

"What is this place?" Bec asked a boy in the crowd.

"This," said the Spanish boy, "is *La Rambla*, one of the most famous streets in Spain. What brings you to Barcelona?"

"I am here to see Paloma Hoyos," said Bec.

"Ah!" the boy said. "The famous flamenco dancer. She is brilliant. She is dancing tomorrow for one of Spain's most respected bullfighters."

He held out his hand and said, "My name is Pablo. One day I hope to be one of Spain's greatest bullfighters."

"Pleased to meet you, Pablo," said Bec. "I'm Bec, and this is my dog, Bronson."

Pablo looked down at Bronson, who was still growling at the human statue.

"He's fiesty, just like a bull," he laughed. "He is *el toro*—which in Spanish means 'bull.' I am on my way to the bullfight now. You are welcome to join me. Perhaps you will see Paloma there watching the fight."

"The bullfight? Classic! I'd love to come!" said Bec.

CHAPTER 4

Paloma Hoyos

Pablo led them through the streets of the city. The cafes were filled with people chatting and eating snacks. They passed art galleries filled with the work of Spanish artists such as Picasso and Salvador Dali. Pablo pointed out odd-shaped buildings that had been designed by a famous Spanish architect named Gaudi.

"Why are most of the shops closed?" asked Bec.

"*Siesta,*" replied Pablo. "In Spain, people go home in the middle of the day. They have lunch with their family. Everyone comes back late in the afternoon and stays until late at night."

They stopped outside an extravagant, half-finished church with huge towers.

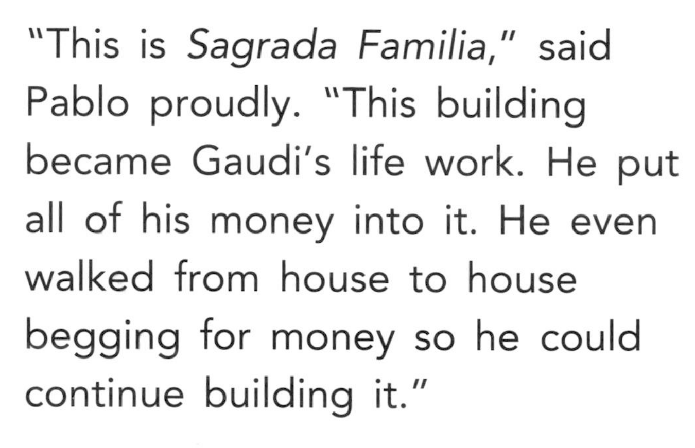

"This is *Sagrada Familia,*" said Pablo proudly. "This building became Gaudi's life work. He put all of his money into it. He even walked from house to house begging for money so he could continue building it."

"It's the biggest church I've ever seen. How long have they been working on it?" Bec asked.

"Nearly 120 years," said Pablo.

Bec crossed the street with Bronson to get a better look at the building. She stood in front of a crowd of tourists.

As Bec went to rejoin Pablo, a black car came around the corner. Bec had a clear view of who was in the car.

"Paloma Hoyos," Bec said softly.

When she reached Pablo, Bec blurted out, "Where's the bullring?"

"Around the corner," said Pablo.

"That was Paloma in the car," Bec cried. "We have to go to the bullfight right NOW!"

Bronson sped ahead, barking a path for them through the crowd. They saw Paloma arrive at the main gate. She was wearing a layered, frilly dress like the one in the photo and a shawl with long, red tassels. Tons of people were waving and calling out, "Paloma! Paloma! Over here!"

She had bodyguards all around her. For a girl getting so much attention, Bec thought, Paloma looked very sad.

Suddenly, Bronson ran forward, barking. He ran straight for the swaying red tassels on Paloma's shawl and bit one. The bodyguards sprang into action.

"Classic," giggled Bec.

"Ah, toro could not help himself when he saw the red tassels," laughed Pablo.

Paloma thought it was funny, too. Her sad eyes lit up as she scooped Bronson up in her arms.

"Your dog is very feisty, just like a bull," she said to Bec and Pablo. "He must see the bullfight. Come inside and sit with us." Then she carried Bronson inside, followed by her bodyguards.

CHAPTER 5

The Bullfight

The late afternoon sun flooded the arena, and families jostled for space and a better seat.

"This is just like going to a football game," whispered Bec to Pablo.

Paloma had reserved box seats. She and Bronson sat right up in front, while Bec and Pablo sat behind the bodyguards. The box seats were some of the best in the house!

The crowd was alive with anticipation. Pablo briefly explained to Bec who was who in the bullfight.

"We call the star bullfighter *matador,* and of course the bulls are—"

"Toros," said Bec with a grin.

"Excellent!" Pablo said.

The crowd cheered as the matador entered. He was wearing tight, black pants, a sparkly vest, and a hat.

The matador flashed a purple and yellow cape in front of the bull to make it charge.

The bull's nostrils flared as it stamped its hoof. Putting its head down, the bull pointed its huge horns at the matador. Its eyes were angry. Then the bull charged. The matador stayed calm. He waved his cape, and right at the last second, he turned. The bull swept quickly past.

The crowd roared. Bec bit her nails. Pablo was on his feet, clapping and cheering loudly. Bronson was barking for the bull. Paloma threw her head back and laughed.

"Paloma likes your dog. He makes her laugh," said Pablo with a grin.

The dance between the matador and the bull went on and on. When the matador or the bull did something extra exciting, a brass band started to play high up in the stands.

Suddenly, a group of men raced toward the bull. They plunged colorful prods into the neck of the bull.

The matador now traded his purple and yellow cape for a red cape and a sword.

It was all getting to be too much for Bec. Finally, the bull was too tired to fight, and the matador killed the bull with his sword. Bec didn't know that the bull was going to die, and she screamed while everyone else cheered.

Pablo tried to comfort Bec by explaining that the bull had been bred to fight and had died quickly. Paloma looked at Bec. It seemed they had traded places. It was Bec who now had the sad eyes.

The bodyguards told Paloma that it was time to leave.

"Come and stay with me," said Paloma, walking past Bec. Bec didn't know what to say.

"Adios, Bec and toro. Thanks for getting me the great seats," said Pablo.

"Don't thank me, Pablo," said Bec, "thank Paloma."

Pablo suddenly turned shy and blushed as he thanked Paloma.

CHAPTER 6

Dancing with Paloma

Paloma lived in a beautiful house just outside the city. As the car pulled up, huge electric gates opened and then closed behind them. Bec noticed that Paloma's eyes were sad again.

"You don't get a lot of time to hang out with your friends, do you?" asked Bec.

Paloma didn't answer. She just played with Bronson. A bodyguard led them to a huge dining hall. There were two places laid out and a bowl for Bronson in the corner.

As they sat down to eat, Paloma said, "This is *paella*. It's a famous Spanish dish of rice, chicken, and seafood. It's my favorite. Try it. You'll like it."

Bec had to admit, it was pretty good.

Paloma turned to Bec and said, "Can you dance?"

"Kind of," said Bec shyly. "I try to dance, but my body just won't do what I want it to."

Bec showed Paloma her sore knee and other assorted scars.

"Nonsense!" said Paloma. "Everyone can dance. All you have to do is feel the music."

"RRRuff! Ruff!" Bronson barked.

"I'll show you," said Paloma, and she turned on some Spanish guitar music. "Dance!" she ordered.

"I'm not used to dancing to this kind of music," said Bec.

"Here," said Paloma, "let's dance together. Follow what I do."

She raised one hand above her head and crossed the other over her body. She spun around and stamped her feet, her head held high.

Bec tried hard to follow, but Paloma moved with such amazing speed. Bec could barely keep her eyes on her. Finally, Bec was too dizzy from all the twirling, and she fell to the ground laughing.

Trying to get her breath back, Bec giggled, "That's classic! I'd love to be able to dance like you. Do you think you could teach me?"

"Sure. First try these." Paloma threw Bec some castanets and showed her how they should sound. Bec put hers on, but all she could make was the "clack, clack, clack" sound of a three-legged horse.

"It's harder than it looks," said Bec.

"It will come with practice," Paloma said with a smile. "Let me show you some dance steps."

Paloma twirled her hands above her head and began to stamp her feet slowly and gracefully. The girls spent hours laughing, dancing, and playing the castanets. Paloma taught Bec the flamenco, and Bec taught Paloma some of her moves. Paloma thought they were hilarious!

"I'm having such a good time," Paloma confided. "It's hard to make friends when I move around so much."

"If you could do one really fun thing, what would you do?" asked Bec.

"Ah, that's easy. I'd run with the bulls tomorrow in Pamplona," Paloma said.

"What? Are you crazy?" Bec had seen the running of the bulls on TV, and it looked dangerous. "You could get really hurt."

"I know. That's why they would never let me. Besides, I have to be here tomorrow to dance. But to do something like that would be such an adventure!" Paloma exclaimed.

Bec remembered the words of her SWAT mission: "Help Paloma Hoyos with her adventure."

"I know a way you could do both," said Bec. "But you can't ask any questions. You can't know how we'll get there and back, and you can't tell anyone. OK?"

Paloma's eyes opened wide. "You would really help me run with the bulls?" she asked.

Bec nodded excitedly.

"Deal," said Paloma quickly.

CHAPTER 7
Run Like Crazy!

The plan was simple. When Paloma was supposed to be resting before her performance, Bec would use the transporter wristbands to get them to Pamplona. Paloma would run with the bulls, and she and Bec would be back by 10 A.M. at the latest. Paloma would have plenty of time to prepare for her performance.

At daybreak, Bec and Bronson snuck into Paloma's room. Bec picked up Bronson and counted down. "Three. Two. One."

Click.

When they landed in Pamplona, people were already lining up for the run.

Paloma was wearing jeans and a T-shirt, and her hair was loose.

"No one will recognize you looking like that!" laughed Bec.

"I'll get going," said Paloma. "I can see the runners lining up."

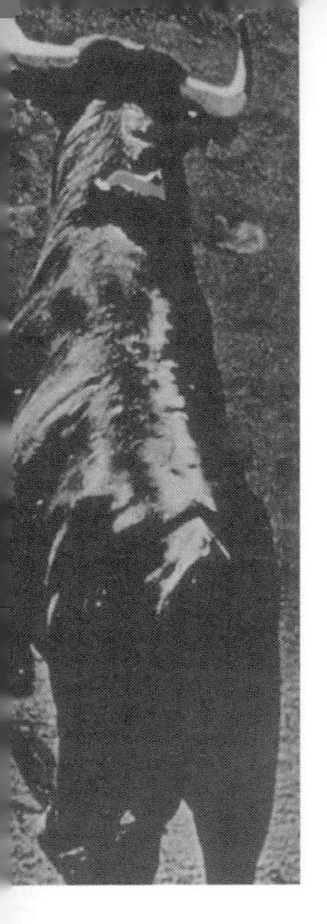

"OK. I'll see you at the end of the run," Bec said. "I think you're insane. Run like crazy!"

Bec gave Paloma a hug for luck. Soon Bec heard the first rocket go off. It signaled the release of the bulls. Not long after, Bec heard the rumble of the runners through the streets.

"Here they come!" she cried.

The stampede of runners and bulls headed toward the arena. Bec and Bronson could see Paloma right in front of the biggest, meanest, fiercest looking bull they had ever seen.

"Run, Paloma!" yelled Bec, her heart racing. Bronson hid behind her legs.

Paloma's leg muscles burned. She could hear the snorting of the bull and feel his hot breath on her neck. She ran and ran, saying to herself, "Faster! Faster!"

Finally, she ran out of the way of the bull and found Bec and Bronson. Paloma was ecstatic.

"Did you see the size of that bull chasing me? That was the BEST thing I've ever done," she said.

"And the craziest!" added Bec.

Bronson gave Paloma a big lick of congratulations.

"We don't have a lot of time. We have to get back," gasped Paloma, still trying to catch her breath.

Bec counted down. "Three. Two. One."

Click.

CHAPTER 8
Back from Pamplona

Paloma barely had time to change out of her clothes and slip into bed before one of her bodyguards came in to wake her. Bec and Bronson quickly hid in the closet.

"Paloma, you must have had a very rough sleep! Your hair is a mess. Hurry and get ready. We must get to the concert hall," he said.

On the way to the hall, Paloma could not stop grinning about her adventure. Bec saw that all of the sadness in her eyes had disappeared. When they got to the hall, Paloma ran straight to her dressing room.

When they were alone, Paloma showed Bec how she darted this way and that to get out of the way of the bulls. Suddenly, she slipped and fell.

"Ouch! I've hurt my ankle!" she cried.

Bec grabbed some ice, but Paloma's ankle was swelling up before her eyes.

"I think you've sprained it," said Bec.

Paloma looked at her ankle and said, "Bec, you're going to have to dance in my place."

"What?" cried Bec. "I can't. I'm not good enough."

"Nonsense. All you have to do is remember what I taught you last night. Feel the music, and dance the flamenco with all of your heart," Paloma said.

There was no time to argue. A bodyguard knocked on the door to tell Paloma that she had 15 minutes to go. Quickly, Bec dressed in Paloma's costume. Paloma did Bec's makeup, pulled back her hair, and slipped on her shoes. The pair looked in the mirror.

"You look fantastic!" said Paloma. "Now just remember how we danced last night, and you'll be fine."

CHAPTER 9
Bec's Flamenco

There was another knock on the door.

"Time to go!" yelled the bodyguard.

Bec walked on stage and waited for the curtain to rise. She was sure she wouldn't remember anything. With the castanets in her hands and her arms above her head, Bec trembled with stage fright.

Then the music started. Almost like magic, her feet and body began to move. Surely this wasn't *her* dancing? She could feel the music! The music was in her, making her dance. Bec danced like she had never danced before. The faster the music went, the faster she danced. She was really dancing the flamenco. She was sensational! She was amazing!

Bec stamped her feet for the last time and swung her arms in the air.

"*Olé*!" she cried.

The crowd went wild, throwing hats and flowers onto the stage. No one knew that it had been Bec dancing. They all thought they had seen the famous Paloma Hoyos dancing.

Back in the dressing room, Paloma helped Bec slip out of her costume and take off her makeup.

This time it was Bec who was ecstatic and talking nonstop. Bronson jumped around and barked.

"I can't believe that was *me* dancing!" Bec said.

"You were ...." Paloma hunted for the word. "CLASSIC!"

They hugged each other and laughed.

There was a crowd at the door wanting to congratulate Paloma on her sensational performance.

"If only they knew," laughed Paloma as she went to greet them, "that it wasn't me at all!"

Someone in the crowd passed Paloma a puppy that looked a lot like Bronson. The tag on its collar said, "To Paloma. Here is your very own 'el toro' so you will never be lonely."

Paloma took the puppy in her arms. "It's so adorable!" she cried. "I must thank the person who gave it to me."

"I bet it was Pablo," giggled Bec.

Just then Bec's wristband started to vibrate. It was a message from Gosic:

Well done, SWAT! Mission complete.

Paloma was busy signing autographs and playing with her new puppy. Bec knew it was time to go. She and Bronson prepared to leave.

"This SWAT stuff is CLASSIC!" Bec said. "Now, if we could just get Gosic to send Zac on a very long assignment to somewhere far away, like Iceland. Wouldn't life be perfect, Bronson?"

"RRufff!! RRRRuff!" barked Bronson.

"If we leave now, I'll have just enough time to get to the dance concert, and I wouldn't miss it for the world now! Say adios to Spain, Bronson. Ready? Three. Two. One."

Click.

MISSION RETURN.

GLOSSARY

adios—(ah-dee-OHS) means "good-bye" in Spanish

castanets—two small shells, usually made of wood or plastic, that many Spanish dancers click between the thumb and fingers

ecstatic—very, very happy

euro—money used by many countries in Europe

feisty—strong and energetic

flamenco—a passionate Spanish dance

matador—the star bullfighter

olé—(oh-LAY) means "bravo" in Spanish

paella—(pie-AY-ya) a Spanish dish of rice, chicken, and seafood

siesta—(see-ES-tah) a rest in the middle of the day, when all of the shops close for lunch

skimmed—read quickly

stampede—an uncontrolled rush of people or animals

toro—(TOR-oh) a bull

ASODOBLE
TE QUIERO
CASCABELES • CAMPANERA • MI JACA • ROCIO
ORQUESTA Y CASTAÑUELAS

ESPAÑA

Levante de Caste
2 de septiembre
5 pesetas
EL MERCANTIL VALENCIANO
PEDRO MUELAS
ñuelas de
paña
MADE IN SPAIN

IT COULD BE YOU!

Secret World Adventure Team

COME TRAVEL TODAY!

MISSION	001	**New York City**	1-4048-1670-4
MISSION	002	**Sent to Sydney**	1-4048-1671-2
MISSION	003	**Lookout London**	1-4048-1672-0
MISSION	004	**Tokyo Techno**	1-4048-1673-9
MISSION	005	**Amazing Africa**	1-4048-1674-7
MISSION	006	**Spectacular Spain**	1-4048-1675-5
MISSION	007	**Incredible India**	1-4048-1676-3
MISSION	008	**Taste of Thailand**	1-4048-1677-1

A complete list of *Read-it!* Chapter Books is available on our Web site:

www.picturewindowbooks.com